BLOOD CRAVING

VAMPIRE MAFIA KINGS 2 (FORBIDDEN FATED MATES ROMANCE)

DRUSILLA SWAN

VAMPIRE MAFIA KINGS SERIES

After a century of war, the world is split into kingdoms ruled by ruthless vampires. When one of them sets their sights on a woman, nothing will stop him from claiming her as his mate. Forever...

Blood Desire (Dominic & Lara)

Blood Craving (Elio & Serafina)

Blood Curse (Ryker & Willow)

INTRODUCTION

Book 2 of the Vampire Mafia Kings series.

As vampire king, Elio must protect his clan at all cost. There's no room for any distraction, especially if it comes in the form of a delicate human witch with a sassy mouth.

On the run from a corrupt government that wants to drain her of her magic, Serafina lands in hot water when she is rescued by a ship full of vampires. She sees the way the vampire king wants to devour her, but he's bitten off more than he can chew if he thinks she's going to melt for him.

Despite the violence she will bring to the gates of his kingdom, Serafina sets Elio's blood on fire, invading his dreams until he is consumed with the need to possess her.

No matter the consequences, he will claim her as his mate. Forever. She will be his, even if it leads to his destruction.

Note: This series takes place about a century after the conclusion of the Doms of Darkness series.

CHAPTER 1

SERAFINA

Keeping my eyes on the ground, I made my way through the crowd of people gathered in the market square. I prayed that nobody could see the outline of the packet of smoked venison I hid under my jacket. My contraband was a small amount, no bigger than my fist, but it would be the first bit of protein that I had to eat in months. My mouth watered in anticipation of biting into the gamey meat. It was also forbidden, as the government only gave regular meat rations to the overseers and protectors, like my employer. Drones like myself only received meat with our rations once a year at Christmas. I was employed as a dishwasher in the home of a gluttonous mid-ranking overseer in the New Boston government. With the daily decadent four-course meals he demanded for dinner every evening, he wouldn't notice the bit of venison I snatched from his kitchens.

Keeping my shoulders hunched, I made my way around the stalls selling overpriced supplies in exchange for the credits we drones received for slaving away in service to our superiors. The wall of muscle I ran into knocked me off balance. I had been so worried about hiding the precious treasure in my arms that I missed the giant man standing in my way. The impact sent me falling back, and I reached my hands out to break my fall.

"Watch where you're going, wench!" growled the dirty man I bumped into. He pulled back his cracked lips in an ugly snarl, stepping menacingly toward me. The packet of meat had fallen out of my arms and landed on the ground during my stumble. I reached for it, but he snatched it out of my grasp.

"What's this?" He pulled loose the twine holding the paper wrapping in place, pausing as he looked at the contents.

"Please, you can have it, just let me go," I whispered.

Realization settled over him and a grin spread across his face, making the scar on his cheek crinkle. He took half of the venison and slipped it into the leather bag tied to his belt.

"The boys at the barracks are going to have a blast with you."

I blanched. Dread settled like a stone in the pit of my stomach. Before I had the chance to react, he grabbed my arm in a painful grasp, wrenching it behind my back as he pulled me to my feet.

"Thief!" he cried out. "Thief!"

As hard as I struggled, I couldn't break out of his grip. In the distance, I heard the commotion of protector soldiers marching toward us, the unmistakable clomp of their boots sounding like thunder as they got closer and closer.

I had to get out of here. Renewing my efforts, I twisted and strained against his hold. A flicker of light in the corner of my eye caught my attention. It was a flame of a lantern. That was my way out of here.

Focusing my mind on the fire, I molded and willed it into a whirling vortex, faster and faster, until the fire spun out of the lantern and whipped toward the sky like a tornado. Screams and shouts echoed in the marketplace as people fled, abandoning their stalls. Even from a distance, the heat singed my face, but I couldn't stop.

"What the fuck is that?" whispered my captor. His grip around my arms grew clammy, shaking with fear. He didn't know what fear was, not yet. I manipulated the fire in my mind, imagining it turning into a fiery serpent ready to strike, and aimed it at the asshole behind me as I dropped to the ground and ducked out of the way of the flames.

I drew my jacket over my head and blocked out his screams as the fire engulfed him head to toe. Sneaking a peek, I watched in horror at the destruction I wrecked. The man was a living fire pillar, his pained cries sinking into my bones as I watched the fire melt him in front of my eyes.

Finally, the life slipped from his eyes, leaving a lifeless charred hunk of flesh that collapsed in front of me. The whirling fire vanished as quickly as it had formed.

It was over, he was dead. I scrambled onto my feet, scanning the carnage of the square. In their haste to escape, the crowds had knocked over stalls and various broken items littered the ground, smashed and trampled by the fearful masses.

"Witch!"

"Seize her!"

My head shot up. The soldiers in their green uniforms were

heading directly in my direction from the other side of the market. There had to be at least a dozen of them.

Ducking behind the stalls, I ran. I cursed myself for losing my temper and using my magic. My mother had always warned me to keep my powers a secret, at all cost. Once the government discovered my powers, they would capture me and drain every bit of magic out of me until I was nothing but an empty vessel. It was what the overseers did to our ancestors after the period of darkness. Stolen magic was what let them establish the settlements. Our magic was still the one thing the overseers needed the most to defeat the vampire gangs that ruled the land outside the settlements.

I had to get out of New Boston. The powers that be were never going to let me go now that they knew I was a witch.

A wooden stall crashed in the distance behind me as the soldiers pushed the obstacle out of their way. I ran into a nearby alley, hoping that I could lose them in the narrow maze of winding paths.

While the men that chased me were bigger and armed, I had the advantage of being nimble and a lifetime of slipping through these alleyways, memorizing each turn and dead end like the veins on the back of my hand.

After turning around multiple corners until I knew I had taken them in a circle, I dashed for my destination. The entire city of New Boston was a fortress, surrounded by tall stone walls that blocked everything but the bare tips of the trees that grew outside the fortified walls. There was only one way out of the city and that was on one of the supply trucks that left the city every night. Once I made it out into the wastelands, I could seek refuge with one of the human rebel factions that were trying to destroy the government.

Thankfully, the protectors hadn't gained any distance on me. A few quick turns down another series of alleys, and I was in the loading area where there was a convoy of trucks loaded with crates of supplies. These were the vehicles going out tonight. To my surprise, there was nobody standing guard. The protectors were trained to keep invaders from coming into the city, keeping someone from sneaking out was not something they were prepared for.

One by one, I peered into the beds of the trucks for a hiding spot, until I found one with a rolled-up black tarp tucked along the side of the wooden crates. I climbed up into the back of the truck and lifted the tarp until I could slide my body under it. The space was just wide enough for me to lie down. Once I was in position on the floor, I pulled the tarp over myself until my entire body was covered.

And then, I waited. The thick tarp blocked out all light, making it impossible to see anything. It seemed like forever until I finally heard voices. I held my breath, afraid that they could somehow hear or see me breathe. After waiting for an eternity, my heart pounded at the chance that they were going to discover my hiding place. Eventually, the trucks roared to life, one by one, and then we were off.

The tarp made it impossible to see where I was being taken, but judging by the jostling of the vehicle, we hadn't gone very far before stopping. Through the hum of the machinery, I heard the sound of crashing waves and the clink of chains. What was going on? Were we at the ocean?

New Boston was a rarity among the human settlements in the Americas because it was the only settlement that had an ocean port. Most access points to rivers and the coasts were vampire controlled, giving them the power to choke off trade routes. This made it impossible for the human government to rapidly expand or challenge the rule of the bloodsuckers.

I was startled as the truck started moving once again, driving uphill for a short distance, before stopping again. We were on a ship, I realized, as the earth swayed beneath me. The only destination I could think of that was also controlled by humans was the prisoner island not too far off the shores of New Boston. It made no sense though, why would there be this many trucks full of supplies going to the island?

The island was home to the most serious threats to the overseers, mostly rebels who planned to bomb the city or overthrow the government. There were also others who were confined on the island. Witches who were discovered and captured by the government. With no way out past the choppy frigid waters, it was the perfect place to make someone disappear once they were drained dry of their magic. Panic set in.

I had to get out of here before we got to the island. Straining my ears, I counted the number of heavy footsteps I heard pacing around the truck where I was hiding. There had to be at least ten men, more than I could fight off or outrun. A loud mechanical rumbling shook the ground, and then the world jerked and rocked. The ship was leaving the port.

Shit.

Now what?

After a while at sea, an explosion rocked the ship. It sounded and felt like a bomb went off, the impact making the vessel shake and rattling my ears. Then, there was a rapid series of six more strikes. I felt the heat before I even lifted the tarp off. We were under attack and the ship was on fire.

The men on board shouted orders as they ran around trying to put out the flames spreading across the deck.

More balls of fire rained from the sky, rocking the ship. The protectors were too busy to notice me as I climbed out of the bed of the truck. Something on the other side of the ship blew up with a loud bang, sending shards of glass and metal flying through the air. I dropped to my hands and knees to shield myself from the debris that showered down. Thick oily black smoke filled the air as the ship tilted sharply, sending everything tumbling to one side. I fell on my butt and slid until my back hit the edge of the deck. Water rushed around me, soaking my clothes.

Fuck. The ship was going to be at the bottom of the ocean by the end of the night.

Gripping the metal wall for support, I staggered to my unsteady feet. My stomach turned as I looked over the edge of the wall. The inky waters churned violently, tossing the ship like it was a toy. In the distance, there was a larger ship that was multiple stories tall and much bigger and faster than the ship I was on. More shots came from that direction.

I had no idea who was on the other ship and why they were attacking, but the enemy of my enemy and all that.

Time to make a choice. Jump in the water and take my chances, or go down with this ship.

I jumped.

The water was shockingly cold, knocking the breath out of my chest. The waves tossed me around like a rag doll. Flailing my limbs, my head bobbed above the surface and I gasped for air. Salty water filled my mouth. Before I could orient myself, the world spun again as a torrent slammed over my head and forced me back under.

The smoke and chaos of the sinking ship faded away, muffled by the dark water. My lungs burned for air as I struggled to claw my way to the surface, but the ocean pulled me deeper and deeper into its depths.

Darkness descended over my vision and my arms and legs grew weak. There was a flush of dizziness and then a sense of contentment washed over me.

This was it. I was going to die.

The cold, dark abyss was going to consume me, and I was ready to accept my fate.

A sharp yank and my world spun again. I landed with a thud on my back. Sputtering, I coughed violently, vomiting up the water I had swallowed. Like a rush of fire, air filled my lungs. Squinting against the bright light shining down from high up above on the masts of the ship, I blinked rapidly as I focused my vision on my rescuer.

I froze. They stood in a semicircle around me, their hungry gazes burning into me as their fangs glistened under the harsh lights.

Vampires.

CHAPTER 2

ELIO

I watched as my men launched another volley of bombs at the human-piloted vessel. Despite the peace treaty between our kind and the humans, the ceasefire only existed when they were secure in their little settlements. Once they ventured out into the wastelands and open waters, they were fair game.

The compass sitting on my desk shook from the impact as we fired once again at the enemy.

It was doubtful that the humans had anything valuable onboard their ship. No, the purpose of the attack wasn't to steal their cargo, but to destroy any hope they had of establishing more sea links between their settlements. The overseers of New Boston were getting far too bold for my liking. Their ability to send a ship out onto ocean waters and maintain a port was already a warning to me. As king of the Diamantis clan territories on the East Coast, I had to nip this in the bud before they started encroaching on more vampire land.

The wide windows of my private cabin spanned the hull of my ship, giving me an open view of the destruction. Thick black smoke billowed in a thick cloud from the human vessel. It wouldn't be long until they were resting peacefully at the bottom of the ocean. I couldn't let a single one of the humans get back to their settlement. A message had to be sent to the overseers, or they would steal everything from my clan in their greedy need for expansion.

While our clan couldn't attack New Boston without violating the treaty, the ceasefire did not apply to the rebel humans who were hellbent on toppling the overseer settlements. Exiled to the wastelands, the rebel forces were a valuable asset in our clan's strategy to keep the overseers in check. By supplying them with weapons and supplies to establish their own colonies, the rebels did the dirty work of terrorizing the overseers and keeping the settlements crippled. Too bad I couldn't supply the rebels with enough weapons to take down New Boston without the risk of them turning on us.

The enemy vessel burst into flame as it split in two and started sinking beneath the surface of the water. This was going to be another grievance that the delegation of overseers was going to bring up at the upcoming interspecies forum. The master of our clan, Dominic, was busy taking care of his new baby, Jasper, and his mate, Lara. In his place, he sent one of his governors, Pedro. Together, the two of us were going to represent the Diamantis clan at the next meeting with the humans.

The meeting was to take place in Iceland, which was werewolf-controlled territory. Since the wolves despised both humans and vampires, it was neutral grounds for the government of overseers and our clan to meet and negotiate.

There was celebratory shouting from the deck below. My men were back, and by the commotion, they must have retrieved something from the sunken ship. I went down to see what was going on.

Like a bunch of drowned rats fished from the ocean, the human soldiers they captured were bound hand and foot. Their soaked bodies shook from the cold wind that whipped across the ship. There were eight of them, strong young men who would provide plenty of fresh hot bloodmeals for my crew while we were out at sea.

To my surprise, there was a smaller figure lying on the deck behind the bulky frames of the protectors we captured. The first thing I saw was the soaking wet mess of curly red hair that fell to her waist.

At that moment, her head shot up, as if she sensed me watching her. Her eyes met mine, sparkling blue and burning with defiance. This was a woman who defied her petite stature and willowy build. There was power simmering beneath the surface. I could feel it humming in the air like an electric field. She wasn't one of the protectors, judging by what she was wearing compared to their green uniforms.

I was intrigued. Our journey to Iceland was going to take days, and I was starving. Ever since Dominic's father, the previous king of the Diamantis clan was poisoned with bagged blood, I only drank fresh from the living, breathing tap. It was the only way to guarantee the blood wasn't tainted. My fangs already itched dropping in anticipation of sinking into her neck.

I signaled to my second in command. "Bring her to me."

"Yes, sir."

"Unharmed," I added.

Nicolas nodded as he went over to retrieve her. Grabbing her by the arms, he heaved her to her feet and dragged her over to me.

"Who are you?" I asked directly. "Or rather, what are you?"

Hatred flashed in her eyes and she turned her head to avoid my gaze.

I snarled. Nobody disrespected me and got away with it.

My hand shot out, gripping her chin in my fingers hard enough to make her gasp in pain as I forced her to look at me.

"I asked you a question."

Even in her powerless situation, she was defiant, her nostrils flaring as she paused before she answered. "Serafina, I was hitching a ride on that ship you blew up. What I am is none of your business."

She was hiding something. I could feel it in my bones. Not that it mattered. What did matter was the fire that she stirred in my belly.

As king of the East Coast, I couldn't let anything or anybody distract me from running my kingdom. That meant I had no time to waste on women, even if the scent of her cut right through my heart of stone. Orange blossom and cinnamon, it was a sweet feminine aroma that wrapped its intoxicating grip around me. My cock hardened in response, straining against my pants, so stiff and swollen, that I could come with just the brush of her fingers against my flesh.

I snarled. This would not do at all. What kind of spell was she weaving over me? It had to be the blood craving, that was all. Too many days out at sea without fresh blood was driving me mad.

There was only one way to cure this sick hold she had on me. Wrapping her hair around my hand, I dragged her closer, wrenching her head aside to expose the milky white column of her neck.

Once I had my fill of her blood, she would be gone and out of my head. The hold this human had over me was a weakness that I couldn't afford. I had to get her out.

My fangs slid into the flesh of her neck like it was a ripe peach. I drank hard and deep, pulling her life force into me. Her pulse quickened, as she struggled and pounded her fists into my chest. She tasted better than she smelled. Sweet with a bit of spice, and a hint of something exotic I had never experienced before. It was heaven. Suddenly, the flavor of her blood changed, taking on a rich sensual flavor. Her hands clenched around the fabric of my shirt, clinging on as she let out a moan. Then, I smelled it, the scent of her arousal joining the metallic tang of her blood.

No fucking way. She was coming to my bite. She ground her body against my aching bulge, riding out her orgasm. It was almost enough to make me bust a nut right there in front of all my men. Her cries of ecstasy turned into keening mewls as she came down from her high. My hunger sated, I sipped delicately from her neck one last time before withdrawing my fangs and sealing the puncture wounds with a swipe of my tongue.

I supported her as I pulled back. She was unsteady on her

feet, her pupils dilated and as dark as the ocean waters under the night sky.

Fuck. That was not how it was supposed to go. Instead of getting my fill of her, I only wanted more. No other blood was going to be good enough. This intoxicating human was my new addiction.

I turned to my men. "Feast! You have pleased me with tonight's attack." Out at sea and with limited supplies, the protectors they captured were nothing but dead weight. The fresh blood would boost the morale of my soldiers. "Toss their corpses overboard when you are finished."

The roaring cries of my men drowned out the ocean waves crashing around our vessel.

I shoved Serafina into Nicolas's arms. "Take her to my cabin and send for the healer. She is to remain unharmed."

Until I figured out what to do with her, no other vampire was going to so much as lay his eyes on her.

She was mine.

CHAPTER 3

SERAFINA

The rats always came at night, scurrying in the walls and across the furniture. Life in New Boston in the reconstruction era was grim and mean. As a citizen drone, I was lucky to have a cot and a job that wasn't at the munitions factory or the brothel. A rat jumped onto the end of my bed and started nibbling at the tips of my toes before scrambling over the threadbare wool blankets up toward my face.

I woke up, bolting to an upright position, the scream dying in my throat. Sitting up, I blinked in confusion in the dark. The bed I was in was unfamiliar and strange. I shivered as the cool air blew across my bare arms.

The lights suddenly turned on, startling me, but there was nobody else in the room. Motion-activated lights.

In the warm glow, I finally got a good look at where I was. My eyes nearly popped out in awe. There were not going to be any rats here, that was for sure. This bedroom was simple, but luxurious compared to the crumbling brick walls of my home. The walls and fixtures were constructed out of polished metal and glass, all materials that were too rare and expensive for even the highest-ranking overseers.

Everything seemed to be electronically controlled, with touchscreens, and buttons. Such a frivolous use of precious electricity. Even the overseer's house I worked in was a humble hovel compared to this place.

Large glass windows curved around the front of the room, giving a wide view of the half-moon glowing in the sky and the ocean waves crashing against the hull of the ship below.

The bedding against my body was smooth and cool against my skin, unlike anything I had ever felt before in my life. As a drone, I was only allowed clothing made from the scratchiest wool and stiffest leather.

My heart raced. It all came back to me, drifting in the ocean, the vampires who rescued me, and then the one with ashen hair who walked with the swagger of someone who owned the place. His gray eyes were burned into my memory as was the piercing pain of his fangs when they sank into my neck. The loose shirt he wore had exposed his chest, revealing a smattering of wiry hair that pressed against me as he fed. He smelled of something herbal, a pleasant spicy scent. It was the same scent that surrounded me in this room.

I reached up to the side of my neck where he drank from me. There was gauze taped there, which I ripped off. To my surprise, the spot under my fingers did not hurt at all. Only two raised bumps revealed what had happened. I frowned. How long had I been unconscious?

Throwing the covers off, I stepped out of bed and wandered around the room. With my fingers, I touched everything I examined, marveling at the delicate craftsmanship and the technology of the gadgets. Some of the items, I realized, were from the before times, when society still had use for leisurely pursuits. In the corner of the room, there was a carved chess set, which I had only ever seen in history books. On the desk, a picture of a tropical island flashed across a laptop screen before changing to a snowcapped mountain. Most of human society didn't have access to a communication network or enough electricity to run computers like this for years.

At the side of the room, behind a frosted glass door, was an actual shower and toilet. Things I had only ever seen in my employer's house. Drones like myself had to make do with a bucket of water from the community well and a washcloth. We were considered lucky if we didn't have to share a bucket.

I looked out the window. There was nothing outside except water all the way to the horizon. The shore was long gone. I had no idea where I was being taken, but it wasn't anywhere near New Boston.

The door at the other side of the room was locked, of course. Not that it mattered, floating in the middle of the Atlantic Ocean, it wasn't like I could escape unless I managed to find a spell to conjure up a set of fins and gills for myself.

By now, I had made a complete circle around the room. My stomach growled, reminding me that the only thing I had eaten since the last morning before work was a bowl of corn and millet porridge. The things I would do for that piece of venison.

As if on command, a panel in the wall next to me slid open, revealing a tray loaded with food. Wisps of steam rose from a bowl of creamy soup, studded with large chunks of vegetables and chicken. Next to the bowl, was a large chunk of bread with a golden crust. I squeezed the piece of bread. The inside was soft as cotton, and the crust crumbled under my fingers with a satisfying crunch. At the center of the tray was a large plate of sliced roasted beef, cooked to a bright pink in the center, unlike the slimy gray meat the government included in our rations. It was covered with some kind of thick gravy which pooled on the plate, soaking into the pile of fried potatoes on the other side of the plate.

The aromatic scent of all this decadent food made my mouth water. I turned my head around, making sure that there was nobody else in the room. This had to be for me, hard enough as it was to believe.

But who was I to ignore a gift that dropped from the heavens? I grabbed the loaded tray and dug into it with gusto as soon as my bottom hit the side of the bed.

No utensils were provided with the food, but that didn't matter. I inhaled the food like I was a starved dog abandoned on the streets, digging in with my bare fingers.

My mouth watered as flavors I had never tasted before exploded on my tongue. Spices and herbs, considered too frivolous by the government to grow on precious farmland, made the food taste divine. The beef fell apart at first bite, tender and soft. I soaked the bread in the juices and gravy that filled the plate, cleaning the surface, and any drops that remained, I made sure to lick clean with my tongue.

With my belly full, my mind began to turn. Despite the comfortable surroundings and delicious food, I was no different from an animal in a cage, fed by an invisible hand. Nothing was free, not in this world. All of this was a gift from the devil, and I was going to pay the price for it eventually.

The sky grew lighter as night turned to dawn. My eyes were

heavy as I watched the sun begin to peek over the edge of the water at the horizon. Suddenly, the air in the room changed.

I spun around and froze at the man standing at the door. It was him, the vampire who drained my blood to the brink of death. He moved silently, slinking from the shadows as he closed the door behind him. The only thing that had given away his presence was his scent. That heady, herbal musk filled my nostrils and made my heart race.

He tapped at the control panel on the wall and blinds lowered from the ceiling to cover the window.

"You can't keep me here."

"Can't I?" His eyes gleamed with amusement. "Where are you going to go? There are at least sixty hungry vampires on the other side of this door. You wouldn't make it ten steps before one of them took their fill of you, and unlike me, they don't have the control to stop before you're dead. This is the safest place you could be on the entire ship."

My mind flashed back to the disgusting creatures that pulled me out of the water. He was right, though I doubted that I was any safer locked in here with him.

He took a step toward me. I matched him by moving back a step.

I lifted my chin. "I won't give you what you want."

Another step. "What do you think I want from you?"

My back hit the wall. I glanced over at the oversized bed in the center of the room.

"You flatter yourself."

My face flushed with heat.

"I'm Elio, by the way. As king of the vampires on this ship, I have little time for the distractions of a woman."

He began to undo the buttons of his shirt, revealing inch by inch his chiseled chest. Sitting on the edge of the bed, he undid the laces of his boots before his hands went to pull down the zipper of his pants.

"What are you doing?" I sputtered. I turned my head away toward the wall, desperate to look at anything besides the dips and lines of his muscled body.

Elio slid under the sheets, covering up everything below his waist. "This is my private cabin. I'm going to sleep. Space is limited on this ship, as we are not used to entertaining guests. This is the only place where you aren't going to be turned into a chew toy, so we're going to have to share a bed."

I gaped at him. Too stunned at his proposal that we sleep in the same bed.

"I promise to keep my hands to myself if you can do the same," he said drily. "Now, if you would please, lay down on your side and let me sleep. It's past my bedtime, and you do not want to be around me when I am sleep-deprived." The last words came out as a growl past his fangs.

I gulped. As grumpy as he could be, this vampire was the only one standing between me and the dozens of blood-thirsty bloodsuckers outside this room. Cautiously, I slid under the covers on the opposite side of the bed, leaving an ocean of space between us until I almost rolled off of the edge.

"Yeah, well, make sure you keep your bits off of me, blood-sucker, or you'll find a stake embedded in your chest." Who knows where my courage came from, but there was no way I was going to let him have the last word. For some reason, this vampire wanted to keep me alive, which meant I had leverage over him.

"Shut up and sleep, human."

Soon, the automatic lights turned off, bathing the room in darkness. I laid there and waited. Just his presence inches away from me was enough to keep me buzzing with adrenaline. As he was a vampire who didn't need to breathe, he didn't snore. The only indication that he had fallen asleep was the release of tension in the air. After what seemed like hours of my mind churning over escape plans, I drifted off into an uneasy sleep.

When I woke up, the room was dim once again, the sun already sinking below the horizon. I must have been exhausted to have slept through the day. To my horror, I found that I had drooled on my pillow. My horror turned to embarrassment when I realized that the pillow wasn't even mine, but Elio's. During the night, I had somehow turned and tossed my way onto his side of the bed. An inch closer and I would have been spooning against his body.

He smirked as I jerked away from him like I had been shocked. "Seems like I should be the one telling you to keep your hands to yourself. You could've just said that you wanted my hot little body," he taunted.

"Ugh!" I tossed the covers back and ran into the bathroom. To my disappointment, the glass door didn't slam behind me but closed softly with some kind of dampening mechanism. Even from behind the bathroom door, I heard his teasing laughter.

I took my time relieving myself and taking a bath with actual hot water and soap. When I came out of the bathroom, he was already gone. On the bed, there was a set of fresh clothes folded neatly into a pile. The outfit was simple, a black shirt and earth-colored pants, but the clothes were still finer than anything I had ever been given in my life. Despite my reluctance to accept anything from a vampire, the rancid unwashed smell from my own clothes was impossible to ignore.

After I changed, I went over and tried to open the main door, but it was still locked. Of course, it was. Elio had another thing coming if he thought I was going to remain locked in here. I picked up the metal framed chair at the desk and threw it with all my strength at the window. It bounced off of the surface with a heavy thud and fell to the floor. There wasn't even a scratch on the window.

There was a crackling sound from the speaker on the desk.

Elio's voice filled the room. "I would appreciate it if you could refrain from destroying my room while I'm busy working."

I looked out the window at the deck below. Elio waved up at me and the bastard dared to wink.

"Let me out of here, you bloodsucking leech!" I screamed.

He spoke into a portable radio unit. "I'll come up and take you out for a walk on the deck after I come home. Until then, I'll send your breakfast up along with some books to keep you entertained. You do know how to read, don't you?"

If looks could kill, that vampire would have been a pile of black dust right now from the glare I shot at him. "Yes, I know how to read. I'm not an imbecile" I hissed out.

"Good, then stay quiet until I come fetch you."

The speaker disconnected before I could curse him out once again.

That was it. This man had another thing coming if he thought he could keep me trapped in this fancy cage and take me out whenever he wanted like a pet.

One way or another, I was going to get off of this ship.

CHAPTER 4

ELIO

Days on the ship were grueling and full of exposure to harsh weather. When word spread of a female human aboard the ship, my men practically drooled like dogs catching onto the scent of a fresh slab of meat. For some reason, the thought of any of them touching, or even looking at Serafina made my vision turn crimson with wild rage.

None of them could be trusted around her. But being locked up with her in cramped quarters was not sustainable. After one day, she was already driving me to distraction. When I came down to the deck, my thoughts were full of her and the feeling of her warm breath on my shoulder as she slept next to me. I didn't detect Nicolas's presence until he cleared his throat loudly in an exaggerated manner.

I startled. That kind of mistake could have cost me my life. It wasn't only the humans that had a price on my head, some of the vampires in my own clan would gladly plant a stake in my chest.

I turned around and nodded at Nicolas.

"Sir, the captain reports that we are on schedule to arrive in Iceland in seven days, though he anticipates rough waters ahead."

"Thank you, Nicolas. Have you learned of any new information about our guest?" I was speaking of Serafina.

Nicolas shook his head in the negative. "I tortured all of the protectors we captured before we disposed of them. None knew of her presence on their ship. She was a stowaway."

Curiouser and curiouser. My instincts were correct that she was hiding something. I had an entire week to get the truth out of her. With a week to break down her resistance, I was going to find out what she was and why she had such a grip on me.

After her tantrum and attempt to destroy my room, I braced myself for confrontation when I opened the door. To my surprise, there was no violence or screaming. Serafina sat there at my desk, reading the book I had sent with her breakfast. Her food sat untouched on the desk, the scrambled eggs dried and crusted over.

I frowned as I closed the door behind me. "You haven't eaten anything today."

"I'm not hungry," she replied without looking up from her book. "I won't be hungry ever again until you release me from this ship. I'm going on a hunger strike."

Resisting the urge to roll my eyes, I grabbed the tray of stale food and put it back in the delivery chute that went directly to the kitchen. Picking up the tablet I used to communicate with my crew, I typed in a request for another meal delivery.

"You know, protein is an extremely scarce resource. That meal could have gone to a starving child."

If my words managed to make her feel guilty about her foolish antics, she didn't let it show.

She flipped a page in the book. "There's nothing worth living for in this world. Starvation would be a mercy for the poor kid."

My jaw clenched. Serafina had a way of pissing me off that nobody else in the world possessed.

Before I could say anything else, the panel on my wall opened, revealing the meals I ordered for the both of us.

I carried the trays over to the desk and dropped one of them in front of her. She shot me a puzzled look as I sat down on the other side of the desk with my own tray.

"I didn't know vampires could eat food." She closed the book she was reading and stood there watching as I twirled some of the creamy pasta onto my fork. "What is that?"

I made sure to make a show of chewing slowly to savor the flavors before I washed it down with a sip of white wine. "Salmon with pasta in a creamy garlic butter sauce," I replied before flaking some of the salmon and taking a bite. "Vampires do not need to eat for sustenance, but we do enjoy the flavors and textures. Besides, I'm only half-vampire."

Her eyes widened. "You're part human?"

I nodded.

She darted her eyes to the plate of dessert on the side.

"That's a molten chocolate lava cake with raspberry preserves."

Serafina's hands tightened around the edge of the desk. "I've never had salmon, or chocolate before, or even raspberries," she whispered. Sending a longing look at her plates of food, she bit her bottom lip.

"You should try it. It's good." There was no way she could resist the temptation for long.

All the slave citizens of the human settlements lived off of tasteless gruel, beans, and rotten foods. That was if they were lucky. The overseers could barely protect their farms supplying those meager rations from the marauding rebels and vampire gangs. On the other hand, the Diamantis clan had a system of greenhouses and indoor livestock breeding centers that our ancestors had established during the dark period. It was more than enough to supply our clan and nourish the humans who lived with us.

She pulled back her chair at the other side of the desk before I even finished my next bite of food.

"Well, maybe I will try some of this." She sat down and picked up the fork, hovering over each plate as if she couldn't decide which one to taste first. "Just once," she mumbled.

I resisted the urge to smirk. It would only piss her off. The important thing was getting her to eat. Mission accomplished. A starving bloodmeal was no good to me.

She picked tentatively at the food at first, taking timid bites as she processed flavors and textures she had never experienced before. Those small bites soon turned into heaping forkfuls. As she chewed, she let out happy noises and little moans of delight. Picking up the wine glass, she gave the contents a cautious sniff before taking a sip. Her lips spread into a smile, and she hummed in approval.

The sounds went straight to my chest, as well as other parts of me. I would catch every last salmon in the rivers and oceans if it would please her. What was wrong with me? I shook my head to clear out the disturbing thought. There was no reason why I should care for her happiness. Serafina was a bloodmeal, a most delicious one, but nothing more. Logically, I knew that, but logic wasn't enough to stop the words from flowing out of my mouth.

"I can arrange for the chef to make something new every day if you would like."

She froze, her fork raised midway in the air and her eyes wide like a deer in headlights, as she contemplated my statement. It would mean giving up her attempts to escape and staying on the ship willingly.

She put down the fork and dabbed at her lips with the table napkin. "How long until the ship reaches its destination?"

"About a week, and then we'll be in Iceland for the meeting with the government."

Her face paled at the mention of her human rulers.

Picking up the wine glass, she took a large swig. "And I will be expected to give you access to my blood in exchange."

"Of course."

For a moment, she played with the napkin in her hands before she nodded. "On one condition."

I tilted my head, intrigued at her bravery. "Name it."

"You will never drain me to the point of unconsciousness, and stop when I tell you to. And this deal is just for the time we are trapped here. All bets are off once we set foot on shore."

Ah, so she was going to run, or at least make an attempt. My mouth watered as I recalled the spice of her blood on my tongue. There was no way I was ever going to let her go. Already, I could feel my fangs itching to descend both in anticipation of tasting her and at the challenge of chasing her. "I accept your terms. Starting now."

I pushed my chair back and reached out for her. "Shall we seal our deal?"

For the first time, she didn't protest as she stood up and walked over to my side of the desk. Once she was within reach, I wrapped my hand around her arm and pulled her closer to me.

As the food had taken the edge off of my hunger, I was going to be gentle this time. I was far too savage with her the first time I took her blood. Bringing her wrist up to my lips, I placed a soft kiss against her pulse point and traced the purple blood vessels with my tongue. Her breath caught in her throat and I felt her heartbeat quicken against my mouth. She was just as affected by my bite as I was by her blood.

The thought was all it took to make my fangs burst forth. They sank in without resistance. Reverently, I sipped at her life force, matching the pull of my mouth with the beat of her heart. She was just as delicious as the first time I tasted her.

And just like the first time, she let out a soft moan as the pleasure spread through her veins. I gathered her weakening form onto my lap and let her ride out her orgasm. She writhed as she came, clenching the back of my neck and one of my thighs in her hands. There was no doubt that her fingers were going to leave bruises. The pain only fueled my hunger.

As she wiggled on my lap, her bottom pressed against my

bulge. This time, I made no attempt to hold myself back, pushing against her as I chased my own pleasure. Tracing my hand over her curves, I reached down to cup her center, pressing her firmly against my body. She let out a mournful cry, so I took pity on her, grinding the base of my palm against her clit. Together we came. I withdrew my fangs, sealing the wound with my tongue.

Sticky with sweat and panting, Serafina pressed her forehead against the crook of my neck. "Is it always like that when you feed from a human?"

I chuckled. "Not often." I wanted to say never, except when a vampire fed from his beloved mate. There was no way I could tell her that. There was no way I could admit it to myself. The possibility of it being true was too frightening. "It must be the loneliness of being stuck at sea," I murmured.

She accepted my answer calmly with a little hum.

The feeding made her weak and it was my fault. I grabbed my tablet and sent a request down to the kitchen for a cup of healing tea.

The tea arrived shortly. I picked Serafina up and eased her back onto my chair.

"Here, drink this. It'll give you your strength back."

She took the mug with both hands and I helped her bring it up to her lips. By the time she drank the last drop, the color had returned to her cheeks and her eyes were bright and alert once again.

"What is this?" she asked. She sniffed the mug and a wrinkle appeared on her forehead.

"It's a healing concoction formulated by our witches, my granny, actually. All the healing powers of spyce without the hangover or the high."

Serafina's eyebrows shot up. "Your grandmother was a witch?"

I smiled and turned the picture frame on my desk toward her. In the picture, a silver-haired woman with a dimpled smile held a chubby baby with a dollop of white hair on top of his head. "Lizzy was one of the most powerful witches of our time. It was her magic that created the spyce plant. Without it, our clan would have lost control and perished once the humans restored sunlight."

"And your grandfather was a vampire?"

I nodded. "One of the greatest soldiers of our clan. He fought in the last war that restored sunlight to the planet. My grandfather was the bravest soldier I knew. He died in battle, just the way he wanted."

She didn't need to know that my grandfather put himself in harm's way, effectively committing suicide after a spell gone wrong used up the last of his mate's magic. My grandmother was his one weakness. In giving up on life after losing his other half, my grandfather also left me stranded and alone in the world.

Over the next several days, I introduced Serafina to various culinary delights. The heady aroma and comfort of a warm cup of coffee was her favorite, while some delicacies, like oysters, were not received as well. But nothing made her face light up like mangoes and pineapples, which came from the Diamantis clan's farms in the southern territories. She finished every meal with a request for a platter of freshly cut exotic fruit, and I could only obey her request. Her joy gave her blood a sweetness that was intoxicating.

Time on the ship passed quickly, and before I knew it, we reached the shores of Iceland.

CHAPTER 5

SERAFINA

My legs shook as I stepped off the ship's ramp onto solid land. Elio kept his arm around my back, keeping me steady as we disembarked. It was late at night, almost twilight. The sky was overcast, with thick heavy clouds that covered the moon. We were at a shipping yard of some sort. The cold and industrial surroundings were a sharp contrast with the warm cozy environment Elio created in his cabin on the ship.

Pedro, Nicolas and several of Elio's guards joined us, keeping their gazes sharp as they scanned the surroundings for threats. In the distance, a vehicle's headlights glowed as it floated closer toward us. Finally, the vehicle stopped in front of us. It was a large black armored car, big enough to fit at least fifteen people. The rear door opened and a large hulking man stepped out.

My breath caught in my throat at the great sight of him. He was almost two heads taller than Elio, and pure muscle. The man's blond hair fell almost to his shoulders and his cheeks were covered in a thick curly beard. Though the sleeves of his jacket covered most of his arm, I could see a thick coating of hair covering his wrists and the back of his hands. Despite his massive size, he moved with the speed and grace of a predator. His eyes had an unnatural golden glow even in the dark of night.

Elio leaned close to me. "Werewolf," he whispered. "Do not panic. They can smell fear."

I gulped. That was easy for him to say.

The man stopped in front of our party and inclined his head in Elio's direction. "Elio, king of the eastern Diamantis territory, welcome. I am Erik, your host for the duration of your stay here."

"Your pack alpha is most generous for allowing us to have this meeting in your country," Elio replied.

"It is to our advantage that all of the species on this planet maintain good relations." Erik tipped his head. I had a feeling the wolves were too proud to do more than that, lest they put themselves in a subservient position.

"I agree. Has the human delegation arrived yet?" Elio asked.

"The humans landed early yesterday morning. They departed from their territory earlier than expected in anticipation of safety issues. Fortunately, their journey was uneventful."

I read between the lines. The overseers were unsure if they were going to be attacked during their journey or if their ship was going to have a mechanical breakdown. That was why I was on the ship that went out. It was a decoy for the real vessel carrying the high-ranking government officials. The overseers were correct to worry that they would be attacked coming to this meeting.

Erik held out his arm and gestured to the vehicle. "Your quarters have been arranged at the palace."

The drive to where we were staying was filled with silence. Tension hung in the air, with nobody willing to speak in front of the wolf.

When we stepped out of the car, the palace was nothing like I imagined it would look like. It was an intimidating, almost evil-looking building. Black and gleaming under the moonlight, it was made entirely of a series of sharp concrete columns reaching up to the sky. Even though I couldn't see any windows in the building, I couldn't shake the feeling that we were being watched.

The pathway from the car to the entrance was lit up with a series of torches. We had only made it halfway down the path when four men stepped out of the building. The man in the center wore a white uniform, the same kind that was worn by the overseer I worked for, except this man had several silver badges pinned to his chest. Flanking him from behind, were three men wearing the green uniforms that all protectors wore.

The eldest protector stood at the rear, his eyes locking onto me. I didn't recognize him, but I couldn't shake the feeling that he was bad news. Shifting my feet, I stepped further behind Elio, hiding behind Pedro and Nicolas. The flames of the torches dimmed before roaring back to life and dancing in the wind.

"Welcome, Diamantis. I am relieved to see you have arrived safely," said the man in white.

Pedro's mouth opened into the beginnings a yawn. When he caught Nicolas and me glaring at him, he swallowed the yawn and looked away sheepishly.

"Premier Walker," Elio greeted. "I appreciate your concern. We have much urgent business to discuss, but it has been a long journey. I propose we wait until the official start of the forum to air our concerns. It will give both of our parties a chance to prepare."

"Of course, I do not wish to keep you waiting for long. Until we meet again."

The humans turned around and disappeared inside the palace.

After that strange encounter, Erik showed our party to our rooms, which according to him, were in a completely separate wing from the humans. The wolves had guards posted at the entrance to our rooms, but Elio preferred to place his own guards to guards.

Even though we were no longer confined to the ship, and thus our deal was null, I was still relieved to find that Elio had arranged for the two of us to share his room. Something about the humans set my nerves on edge.

My eyes grew heavy, and a yawn escaped my lips despite my attempt to hold it in.

"Sleep, Serafina." Elio brushed his lips against my forehead. "We have a couple of days until the meeting begins. I would like to show you around Iceland tomorrow."

True to his word, Elio had Erik take us on a drive around Iceland's most famous sights. From the volcanoes and lava fields to the black sand beaches, I saw so many things I had only read about in books. The giant waterfall with the stream of water lit up by the almost full moon was the most impressive sight, but the way Elio held his jacket over my head to shield me from the spray of moisture was what I was going to remember long after the end of this trip. Tired and wet from our hike to the waterfall, Erik took us to a charming fishing village to try the local cuisine. Colorful cottages and fishing huts dotted the rocky landscape. It was so peaceful and idyllic that it resembled something straight out of an old fairy tale.

As it was early in the evening, the shops and restaurants were still open. Even though I was wearing Elio's jacket, a gust of wind made me shiver. He spotted a stall selling fur hats and purchased a gray sealskin hat for me. Elio placed the hat gently on my head, tucking my hair behind my ears. The warmth from his actions filled my chest and chased away the chill of the night air.

"A lovely choice for your lovely wife, sir," said the stall owner.

I blushed at the seller's words, but I did not have the energy to correct him. His eyes had the same golden glow as Erik's eyes. Another wolf.

We strolled along the street, perusing the windows of the shops and restaurants. "Are all the inhabitants on this island werewolves?" I asked Elio.

"Yes. The original wolf population escaped from their enclave in Huntington Harbor at the start of the dark period. Over time, they intermingled and bred with the local population on this island. While the rest of the world burned and destroyed each other, they defended Iceland against invaders. All the people still living here are their descendants. They get to play both sides, getting the resources they need from the outside world from both the humans and the vampires."

I sighed. "It's so peaceful here. I wonder if this was what the human settlements could have been in the reconstruction if the overseer warlords were not corrupted by their need for power."

Across the street, I noticed a food stall with a line of patrons snaking along the sidewalk. A delicious smoky aroma wafted over.

Elio tugged my hand and led me to the stall. "Come, let's see what the local delicacies are on this island."

After we had our fill of the most delicious smoked fishcakes, we stepped into the bar next door to try the Icelandic beer. The decor inside resembled a medieval castle, more than a quaint fishing village. The interior was dark, with thick stone walls and worn wooden tables. Candles illuminated the bar in a warm golden glow. Elio and I were on our second beer when trouble found us.

Two protector soldiers, no older than I was, crashed drunkenly into our table. As soon as they saw me, their demeanor changed, a predatory gleam coming into their eyes. "Hey, sweetcheeks. Let us buy you a drink. We'll show you what it's like to be fucked by two real men!" They chuckled at their lewd pickup line.

The flames of the candles roared to life, singing the ceiling.

Quicker than I could follow with my eyes, Elio grabbed them by their shirts and tossed them across the room. The men's bodies hit the stone wall with a sickening thud, their bones cracking on impact. In a flash, Elio leaped across the bar, landing on top of their bodies. He finished them off with a final twist of their necks.

The bar fell silent.

I placed my hand on his shoulder. "Elio, no."

Elio shrugged off my touch. I gasped when I saw his face. Not only were his fangs fully descended, but his eyes were blood-red with anger. There was little of the man who introduced new things to me with gentleness. Only the monster remained.

"You can't," I whispered.

He snarled, revealing his sharp teeth. "You dare defend them?" His fangs distorted his words.

"No, but think of your clan. The meeting. These jerks were part of their delegation. This could start a war."

His shoulders heaved with repressed rage, but my words reached him.

In one move, he swept me into his arms. "We're leaving. Now!"

CHAPTER 6

ELIO

I was fully aware that there would be a price to pay for my outburst at the bar.

"What is the meaning of this, vampire?" The Premier's voice roared through the grand meeting room of the palace as he pushed the doors apart and stormed into the room. He was joined by two of his protectors, including the older one who greeted us on the night we arrived in Iceland.

A gust of cold air blew into the room, making the flames in the oil lanterns flicker and dance wildly.

The official start of the forum wasn't supposed to be until the end of the week, and I was already on the brink of inciting war between the Diamantis clan and the human government.

My men and my mate were gathered at the meeting table, as today was our day to use the meeting room. My guards sprang into action, raising their weapons at the intruder.

I held up my hand in a gesture for them to stand down.

I feigned boredom as I addressed him. "Premier Walker, may I suggest that you employ soldiers who have at least matured past the worst of their adolescent hormones the next time you meet with us? Your grunts disrespected my mate and threatened her life."

The Premier sputtered. "There will be no negotiations. The forum is canceled!"

The older protector rushed to salvage the situation. Judging by the stripes and badges on his uniform, he was a general. "Now hold on. Let's not be hasty. We have no way to confirm what happened, but we do have eyewitnesses to the murder of two of our men. I believe that we can fix this situation. An eye for an eye. Give us one of your men in exchange and we will consider this matter finished."

The general's eyes locked on Serafina.

"We can take the woman. She's one of ours anyway."

My mate's hands clenched around mine. Through our bond, I sensed her fear.

"Over my dead body," I growled. I was ready to spring out of my seat and rip his head off, peace treaty be damned.

The Premier scoffed. "Surely you're not going to risk a declaration of war over some warm pussy?"

Enough was enough.

It was hard to tell which side pulled their weapons first, but a shot from the protector's plasma gun went wide, shattering the windows in the room.

Pulling Serafina with me, I ducked under the table to escape the first rays of sunlight rising from the horizon.

To my surprise, I saw my mate chanting with her eyes closed. I had no idea what she was doing, but it soon made sense.

The flames of the lantern encircled the room. As the fire formed a ring and spun around, it grew in size, until the entire room was surrounded in the eye of a fire tornado.

"What the fuck is going on?" uttered one of the humans.

This was Serafina's secret and why she had been running away from the humans. My mate was a witch.

The fire spun faster and faster until it shrunk around the general.

His screams gurgled in his throat, turning into a whimper as the fire consumed him. That whimper soon turned into silence. The man's crisp and charred body fell to the ground.

Serafina emerged from under the desk. "I suggest that you reconsider your tone and position the next time you speak with any members of our clan at the forum. This was your last and final warning. Do you understand?"

"Y--yes," he stuttered. The Premier's legs shook as he backed out of the room.

She dropped to her knees next to me. "Did I fuck up your negotiations?"

I gathered her in my arms and placed a kiss on the top of her head. "Not at all. You were brilliant. Those men had bad intentions this whole time. You put them in their place, and they'll think twice before crossing us in the future."

Erik rushed into the meeting room and surveyed the damage. "Fucking humans and bloodsuckers, always squabbling like toddlers." He rushed to the windows and pulled down the blackout curtains. "I leave you guys alone for an hour and you destroy the place."

With the room shrouded in darkness once again, we emerged from under the table. "Sorry, Erik. I'll pay for the damages."

"You bet your ass you will," he grumbled. "Is the forum still going to take place?"

I nodded. "Yes. Give the humans time. They can't afford not to negotiate."

Erik resumed mumbling curses under his breath as he stormed out of the room.

Serafina pulled out of my arms. "Do you still want me, now that you know the truth?"

What a ridiculous question. The frustration made me growl. "Of course I do. This changes nothing."

I punched the table.

"For fucks sake. I love you, Serafina. I tried to fight it because it was safer to remain alone, but it was futile. You give my life hope and purpose. I was nothing but a shell before you arrived."

Tears shimmered in her eyes as she looked at me. "I love you, too, Elio."

Gathering her in my arms, I wrapped her tightly in my grasp and vowed to never let her go.

CHAPTER 7

ELIO

I was fully aware that there would be a price to pay for my outburst at the bar.

"What is the meaning of this, vampire?" The Premier's voice roared through the grand meeting room of the palace as he pushed the doors apart and stormed into the room. He was joined by two of his protectors, including the older one who greeted us on the night we arrived in Iceland.

A gust of cold air blew into the room, making the flames in the oil lanterns flicker and dance wildly.

The official start of the forum wasn't supposed to be until the end of the week, and I was already on the brink of inciting war between the Diamantis clan and the human government.

My men and my mate were gathered at the meeting table, as today was our day to use the meeting room. My guards sprang into action, raising their weapons at the intruder.

I held up my hand in a gesture for them to stand down.

I feigned boredom as I addressed him. "Premier Walker, may I suggest that you employ soldiers who have at least matured past the worst of their adolescent hormones the next time you meet with us? Your grunts disrespected my mate and threatened her life."

The Premier sputtered. "There will be no negotiations. The forum is canceled!"

The older protector rushed to salvage the situation. Judging by the stripes and badges on his uniform, he was a general. "Now hold on. Let's not be hasty. We have no way to confirm what happened, but we do have eyewitnesses to the murder of two of our men. I believe that we can fix this situation. An eye for an eye. Give us one of your men in exchange and we will consider this matter finished."

The general's eyes locked on Serafina.

"We can take the woman. She's one of ours anyway."

My mate's hands clenched around mine. Through our bond, I sensed her fear.

"Over my dead body," I growled. I was ready to spring out of my seat and rip his head off, peace treaty be damned.

The Premier scoffed. "Surely you're not going to risk a declaration of war over some warm pussy?"

Enough was enough.

It was hard to tell which side pulled their weapons first, but a shot from the protector's plasma gun went wide, shattering the windows in the room.

Pulling Serafina with me, I ducked under the table to escape the first rays of sunlight rising from the horizon.

To my surprise, I saw my mate chanting with her eyes closed. I had no idea what she was doing, but it soon made sense.

The flames of the lantern encircled the room. As the fire formed a ring and spun around, it grew in size, until the entire room was surrounded in the eye of a fire tornado.

"What the fuck is going on?" uttered one of the humans.

This was Serafina's secret and why she had been running away from the humans. My mate was a witch.

The fire spun faster and faster until it shrunk around the general.

His screams gurgled in his throat, turning into a whimper as the fire consumed him. That whimper soon turned into silence. The man's crisp and charred body fell to the ground.

Serafina emerged from under the desk. "I suggest that you reconsider your tone and position the next time you speak with any members of our clan at the forum. This was your last and final warning. Do you understand?"

"Y--yes," he stuttered. The Premier's legs shook as he backed out of the room.

She dropped to her knees next to me. "Did I fuck up your negotiations?"

I gathered her in my arms and placed a kiss on the top of her head. "Not at all. You were brilliant. Those men had bad intentions this whole time. You put them in their place, and they'll think twice before crossing us in the future."

Erik rushed into the meeting room and surveyed the damage. "Fucking humans and bloodsuckers, always squabbling like toddlers." He rushed to the windows and pulled down the blackout curtains. "I leave you guys alone for an hour and you destroy the place."

With the room shrouded in darkness once again, we emerged from under the table. "Sorry, Erik. I'll pay for the damages."

"You bet your ass you will," he grumbled. "Is the forum still going to take place?"

I nodded. "Yes. Give the humans time. They can't afford not to negotiate."

Erik resumed mumbling curses under his breath as he stormed out of the room.

Serafina pulled out of my arms. "Do you still want me, now that you know the truth?"

What a ridiculous question. The frustration made me growl. "Of course I do. This changes nothing."

I punched the table.

"For fucks sake. I love you, Serafina. I tried to fight it because it was safer to remain alone, but it was futile. You give my life hope and purpose. I was nothing but a shell before you arrived."

Tears shimmered in her eyes as she looked at me. "I love you, too, Elio."

Gathering her in my arms, I wrapped her tightly in my grasp and vowed to never let her go.

EPILOGUE

ELIO

After Serafina put the fear of mortality into Premier Walker, he came to the negotiating table with a much more subdued demeanor.

The negotiations between our parties were long and drawn out, but eventually, we came to terms that were agreeable to both humans and vampires. The humans agreed to cease establishing new colonies for the next year. In exchange, the Diamantis clan would stop attacking their convoys as they traveled through the wastelands.

It didn't matter in the grand scheme, as there were other vampire gangs as well as human rebels who would take our place in looting their trucks.

What was important was that we got our desired outcome, a stop to their colonies popping up next to our territories like weeds.

After the forum concluded, we boarded the ship once again. I couldn't wait to get back to my kingdom and show Serafina around.

I was sitting resting on deck, with Serafina in my arms as we watched the waves crash against the shore. Glancing impatiently at Nicolas, I signaled to him to hurry it up. Why weren't we leaving port?

Nicolas ran over. "Sir, we seem to have a problem. Pedro is missing."

I had a sinking feeling about this, but it was a matter that had to be discussed with my master when I got home.

"Is there anything else, or anyone else?" I asked.

Nicolas shook his head. "No, sir. Just him and the things he had in his cabin."

"We can't wait any longer. Tell the captain to set sail. Wherever Pedro is, he'll have to find his own way home."

ONE YEAR LATER

I ended the virtual meeting with Dominic and shut down my computer.

Our worst suspicions were confirmed. Pedro was spotted by our spies in Europe along with a sudden influx of spyce to the region. He was the one smuggling our drug into the region under our noses the entire time.

As he was currently under the protection of the Federov clan, he was out of our reach for the time. But a rat was trusted by nobody. Once they grew suspicious of him our clan would get our vengeance.

I went downstairs to the kitchen area to see how far dinner preparations were coming along.

Ever since Serafina discovered she was pregnant with our daughter, she challenged our chef with the most unusual food cravings. Most recently, she craved mangoes and pickles dipped in chili pepper flakes and caviar.

The look on our chef's face told me all I needed to know. I shot her an apologetic look. "Thank you for indulging Serafina. This must go against all of your culinary training."

Chef shook her head as she added the final spoonful of caviar pearls onto a slice of seasoned mango. She wiped down the edge of the plate and pushed it in my direction. "I know better than to judge a pregnant woman for what her child demands she eats. If this abomination is what it takes for you to have a healthy baby and a happy mate, then so be it."

My beautiful pregnant mate greeted me with a smile, which turned into a beaming grin when she spotted the offering in my hands.

"Gimme!"

I chuckled as I set the plate on the bed next to her. "Greedy little minx." Placing a kiss on the top of her head, I fluffed the pile of pillows behind her back and helped her sit upright.

As she ate, I placed my ear on her swollen belly and massaged her taut skin, hoping for a response from our unborn daughter.

Her impending birth filled my soul with hope and joy. This was a fresh start. The next generation would have a better childhood than I did, at least a mommy and daddy who loved each other, and relative peace in the world.

Suddenly, I felt a kick against my palm. My head shot up, and I looked at Serafina in shock. "She recognizes me!" At that moment, I vowed that I would never abandon my girls and that I would do everything in my power to ensure that my daughter lived a happier life than I did.

Thank you for read Blood Craving

GET THE NEXT BOOK IN THE SERIES: Blood Curse (Ryker and Willow's story)

FREE BOOK: SOLD TO THE MASTER VAMPIRE

The Doms of Darkness series begins with Alex and Amanda's story in Sold to the Master Vampire.

ONE CLICK TO GET Sold to the Master Vampire for FREE
GET THE COMPLETE SERIES: Doms of Darkness (The Complete Series: Books 1-4)
A master vampire takes what he wants, when he wants it.
The moment I saw her, I knew I had to have her.
The perfect pet.
Mine to tame. Mine to pleasure. Mine to protect.
A woman I could mold into my future queen.
But she's not as helpless as she seems.
Will she take her place as my mate?
Or will she lead me to my destruction?

I pushed my half-eaten chocolate raspberry mousse cake away and collapsed against the back of my seat. "I can't possibly eat another bite." The café where we had staked our claim smelled like dark roasted coffee, sugar, and cigarette smoke. I looked out the window and gazed lazily at the fashionable men and women walking down the street. They were so lucky to live here.

"You're such a lightweight, Amanda. Gimme." Meghan reached across the table and grabbed my plate. "I never want to leave Paris," she mumbled around a mouthful of mousse.

I don't know how she did it. We met at the hostel last week, and ever since then all we had done was sight see and eat. My new best friend and I had a plan to eat our way across the city before moving on to the next country on our Euro trip, where we were going to do the same thing all over again. While most tourists came to Paris for luxury shopping, we were here for the food and whatever tourist traps we could sneak into on a backpacking budget.

Suddenly, Meghan let out an ear-piercing scream. Her fork clattered to the floor, and she knocked over her cup of coffee. She clutched at her throat. Panic filled her eyes.

"Meghan!" I tried to reach across the table, but my arms moved like they were filled with lead. Her mouth opened and closed, but no words came out. Blood sprayed out between her fingers. The mist of blood splattered onto my face.

I jerked awake, falling back to reality from my dream of a life that didn't exist anymore. Every muscle and bone in my body ached from sleeping on the cold concrete floor. My stomach threatened to turn itself inside out from the smell of piss, blood, and vomit. Screams from several cells down the hall from mine bounced off the stone walls in a never-ending echo. There was a sickening thud and then it was silent.

My cellmate covered her ears and rocked back and forth with her head between her knees. I stood up on my tiptoes and peered out of the tiny street-level window in our cell.

It was futile, of course. Time had no meaning in this place. Once the vampires figured out how to get rid of the sun, it became impossible to tell how much time had passed. Even the moon disappeared without light from the sun. With nothing to light up the inky black sky, eternal darkness took over the world.

Keys jangled, and a metal door screeched in the distance. The hairs on my arms stood up in warning.

Not again.

I crawled back to the far corner of the cell and shrank down into the shadows as low as I could. I wrapped my arms around my knees and buried my face in my knees. If only the stone walls would swallow me up, so I could disappear. Silently, I prayed that they would ignore me and walk past my cell.

Heavy footsteps clomped down the hall, closer and closer. I made out two sets of footsteps. The guard who watched over the prisoners walked with a shuffling gait. The customer looking to buy a human from the merchandise on display in the dungeon walked with steady, sure steps. The human captives here were being sold off to vampires like cattle to be slaughtered. Whose turn was it going to be today?

The footsteps stopped suddenly. Male voices mumbled too softly for me to make out what they were saying. They were standing on the other side of the door.

I held my breath until my head pounded. Maybe if I kept perfectly still, they wouldn't see me.

"That one."

No, no, no, no.

The squeaky lock turned, and my cell door swung open with a groan. The guard came in first, followed by another vampire, who I guessed was today's buyer.

I darted my eyes around the room, looking for an escape route, but the two demons blocked the only way out of the room. The space closed in on us. Their large bodies took up all the room in the tiny cell.

The buyer was stylishly dressed, in a well-tailored gray silk suit that must have cost more money than I had in my bank account. His strong features were closed, revealing nothing about him. If I didn't know that he was a monster, I would have said that he was the most beautiful man I had ever seen.

The burly guard grabbed me by my arms and hauled me to my feet. I struggled, but it was less than useless. In fact, my resistance seemed to excite him. The demon tightened his grip painfully around my arms and flashed his fangs in my face. The smell of raw blood and decay was overwhelming. I was smelling the scent of his last meal. A captive just like me. My stomach turned violently. I wrenched myself out of his grasp and threw myself against the wall.

"Filthy whore!" The vampire guard growled and raised his hand to hit me. I squeezed my eyes shut, but the painful blow never came.

I opened my eyes and saw the guard's feet floating above the ground. The buyer had one hand wrapped around the guard's throat. The buyer flashed his fangs and his copper eyes glowed as he squeezed the guard's neck. Bone and tissue ground together, the noise echoing in the cell. Even though vampires didn't need to breathe, their flesh still bruised and their bones still broke. The guard clawed uselessly at the hand around his neck.

"You do not ever touch what is mine," he rasped around his fangs. He threw the guard to the other side of the room. My heart thudded at his strength and speed. His movements were quick, almost too quick to be seen with the human eye. The guard must have weighed over two hundred pounds, but the buyer tossed him aside like a crumpled ball of tissue without messing up his expensive suit. Despite his refined and regal exterior, there was no doubt that he was a warrior. A killer draped in fine silk.

"I-I'm sorry, Master Diamantis." The guard started to get up, but one look from the master vampire had him down on his knees again. The guard kept his eyes on the ground and bowed his head to the floor as he spoke, "She is to your satisfaction, Master?"

The master vampire paused to examine the goods he was buying. He swept his eyes up and down my body. Crossing my arms, I hugged my stomach. Though I could not imagine why. What he saw must have satisfied him.

"She will do. Have your sire arrange the settlement with my men."

"Yes, Master, anything you command." The guard cowered and bowed his head in subservience and backed out of the cell. Without giving me another glance, he backed out of the cell. He tripped over his feet, eager to get away from the powerful vampire.

I was all alone with the buyer now. Fear chilled my blood. I looked up into the cold, stony eyes of the vampire who bought me.

The vampire who was now my owner. My master. He was going to own and use me, and I was going to obey.

Or at least that's what I was going to make him think. As soon as I had a chance, I was going to make my escape.

GET SOLD TO THE MASTER VAMPIRE FOR FREE!

GET THE COMPLETE SERIES: Doms of Darkness (The Complete Series: Books 1-4)

DOMS OF DARKNESS SERIES

In a world of eternal darkness, humans are nothing more than chattel and vampires rule with an iron fist.

Sold to the Master Vampire (FREE AT YOUR FAVORITE RETAILER) (Alex & Amanda)

A Pet for the Master Vampire (FREE only available at www.drusillaswan.com/newsletter) (Alex & Amanda)

Captured by Her Vampire Mate (Grant & Lizzy)

Mated by the Warrior Vampire (Dante & Rose)

Tamed by Her Vampire Protector (Leo & Meghan)

GET THE COMPLETE SERIES: Doms of Darkness (The Complete Series: Books 1-4)

VAMPIRE MAFIA KINGS SERIES

After a century of war, the world is split into kingdoms ruled by ruthless vampires. When one of them sets their sights on a woman, nothing will stop him from claiming her as his mate. Forever…

Blood Desire (Dominic & Lara)

Blood Craving (Elio & Serafina)

Blood Curse (Ryker & Willow)

MATING SEASON SERIES

These alpha wolf pairs will stop at nothing to claim their mate when they catch her scent. She's in heat and ripe for breeding...

SERIES BOX SETS

Mating Season Collection 1 (Books 1-3)

Mating Season Collection 2 (Books 4-6)

Mating Season Collection 3 (Books 7-9)

Owned by the Billionaires (FREE at your favorite retailer) (Fiona, Huxley, Derek)

Trick or Treat with the Billionaires (FREE only available at drusillaswan.com/newsletter) (Fiona, Huxley, Derek)

MATING SEASON SERIES

Captured by the Billionaires (Josephine, Samuel, Liam)

Mated to the Billionaires (April, Evan, Lawrence)

Kidnapped by the Billionaires (Sophie, Rick, Owen)

Stranded with the Billionaires (Amber, Nicholas, Constantine)

Taken by the Billionaires (Sarah, Mac, Callum)

Sold to the Billionaires (Beth, Troy, Sebastian)

Given to the Billionaires (Penny, Jake, Duncan)

Claimed by the Billionaires (Scarlet, Paxton, Austin)

ALSO BY DRUSILLA SWAN

If you want more by Drusilla, but you're not sure what to read next, here's a handy guide to help you pick your poison…

DOMINANT ALPHA MALES

All of my books

VAMPIRES

Doms of Darkness Series

Vampire Mafia Kings Series

Alien Vampires of Sangloria Series

MFM MENAGE

Mating Season Series

WEREWOLVES

Mating Season Series

BILLIONAIRES

Mating Season Series

Indebted to the Billionaire Series

BRATVA MAFIA

Indebted to the Billionaire Series

ABOUT DRUSILLA SWAN

Steamy. Over-the-top. Alphas who claim their mates. Satisfying happily-ever-afters.

Join my newsletter at drusillaswan.com to get freebies and updates.

Find Drusilla at:

drusillaswan.com

Sign up for Drusilla's newsletter at:

drusillaswan.com/newsletter

Like Drusilla Swan on Facebook:

facebook.com/drusillaswan

Follow Drusilla Swan on Instagram

instagram.com/drusillaswanauthor

- facebook.com/Drusilla-Swan-110213218122378
- instagram.com/drusillaswanauthor

This is a work of fiction. Any resemblance to actual persons, living or dead, business establishments, events or locales is entirely coincidental. All rights reserved. Except for use in a review, the reproduction or use of this work in any part is forbidden without the express written permission of the author.

Copyright © 2024 by Drusilla Swan.

All rights reserved.

❀ Created with Vellum

Milton Keynes UK
Ingram Content Group UK Ltd.
UKHW042140281024
450365UK00001B/19